This book belongs to:

_____

_____

_____

First US edition 2022

Library of Congress Catalog Card Number 2021953476
ISBN 978-1-5362-2857-1

22 23 24 25 26 27 CCP 10 9 8 7 6 5 4 3 2 1

Printed in Shenzhen, Guangdong, China

This book was typeset in Lucy Cousins.
The illustrations were done in gouache.

Candlewick Press
99 Dover Street
Somerville, Massachusetts 02144

www.candlewick.com

Maisy's Snowy Day

Lucy Cousins

CANDLEWICK PRESS

One day, Maisy wakes up to a wonderful surprise. It's snowing!

After breakfast, she gets ready and puts on her coat, hat, scarf, gloves, warm woolen socks, and boots.

Brrr, it's very cold outside!

The snow on the ground
is soft and scrunchy.

Maisy puts seeds out for
the hungry birds to eat.

Scrunch
Scrunch
Scrunch

It's time for Maisy to go to the park to meet her friends.

Her boots leave footprints in the snow as she walks along.

Eddie and Cyril are trying to catch snowflakes as they fall.

Maisy and Tallulah roll the snow into big balls.

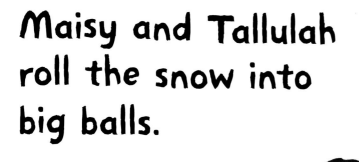

Cyril and Eddie put the snowballs on top of each other.

Charley finds twigs for whiskers and pebbles for a nose, eyes, and mouth.

It's a snow Maisy!

Eddie blows snow with his trunk as they climb up a big hill.

It's time
for a sled race.
Watch out for the bumps!

Oh dear, now Cyril is cold. Maisy gives him a great big hug.

The sun is setting and it's getting dark in the park. Time to go home.

Maisy's house is covered in twinkly lights that shine brightly in the dark. It looks so pretty! Maisy invites everyone inside.

All the friends are cozy and happy together. Maisy makes hot chocolate, the perfect treat to end a lovely, snowy day!